THINGS I DO WHEN I'M AWAKE

Will Viharo

THRILLVILLE
PRESS

Seattle, WA

THINGS I DO WHEN I'M AWAKE
Copyright 2016 Will Viharo

Original cover art by Dyer Wilk – aseasonofdusk.com

Formatting by Rik Hall – WildSeasPress.com

ISBN: 978-0692803479

First Printing

Printed in the United States of America

Published by Thrillville Press

www.thrillville.net

1 0 1 1 2 0 1 6

"If you have a dream of a dog walking and you are the one walking the dog then this means that you feel like you are really in charge of something and getting a lot of things done. You feel like you have been put in charge and you are in control of whatever you are working on currently. Be happy with this outcome. As long as you are a good person you will get through this well. If you have a dream in which you see a dog walking as if it were a person then this means that you are going to deal with something of an improbable nature soon. Something that you never thought could happen or occur is now going to happen so you need to be ready for it or it will be even more shocking."

Gotohoroscope.com

"Is all that we see or seem
But a dream within a dream?"

Edgar Allan Poe

For Miss Houston 1960

Neon Reflections

I am not sure if this is a dream, my imagination, or a memory. It doesn't matter anymore. The distinction has become irrelevant.

It looks like a scene from an old movie, or a classically American painting: the el tracks with the rollicking trains, their lighted windows like beads of fire in a distant horizon, the full moon glowing in the cold, raven-blue night sky with aloof omniscience, and the diner with its neon sign reflecting shimmering high-tech rainbows on the rain-slick streets.

I'm purposely romanticizing the scene because this is how I envision my entire life, like a surreal portrait, a cinematic still life that moves almost imperceptibly, changing characters, shifting settings and time so deftly that it is only in hindsight that I realize I'm not where, or who, I used to be only a few moments ago.

In a world that makes no sense at all, this makes all the sense in the world.

Right now, at this very second in time and space, I'm walking past the Bay Diner off New Utrecht and 18th Avenue in the Bensonhurst section of Brooklyn, New York. It's maybe 10pm or so, but again, I have no sense of time anymore. Only light and darkness.

I do know I'm on my way to my mother's apartment nearby. I walk slowly past the diner because I'm not sure if I want to go in and sit at the counter with some coffee and pastry and maybe a smile from a sympathetic waitress, or if I want to just go home and see Mother, who is probably waiting up for me, pacing like a caged panther.

Alluding to one's mother as a hungry carnivore may strike some as being tasteless. I don't mean it to sound offensive.

It's just that I hardly know the woman. You see, we just met a few days ago.

I close my eyes, then open them again. I'm still here. Wherever this is. Whoever I am.

I hear a train pass overhead. A chill breeze sends signals of reality down my spine. No one else is around. The streets are eerily silent. I'm all alone with this strange woman who was once an official beauty queen. In fact, she was voted Miss Something Or Other, wherever she's originally from, many dark moons ago. Then she went to New York City, my birthplace, as an aspiring, promising actress. There she met my father, whoever he was. They had a one-night stand. I was conceived. Then the madness set it. Perhaps there's a connection, biological or otherwise, I don't know. I may even have inherited it, and it will strike me latently as it did her, though I've read that schizophrenia skips a generation. I'm her direct descendent, her only child, even if it was all only an accident of indifferent fate.

She is the most tragic person I've ever met. That's all I know for sure.

I decide not to go back to her place right away. I need some space to breathe. I go into the Bay Diner. The ambience reeks of middle-class Mafia. The nonchalant rudeness but down-to-earth honesty of New Yorkers suits my cynical nature. At least my mother can walk around safely in the middle of the night, since she has trouble sleeping, and buy herself cigarettes at the local corner market, which never closes. An Arab immigrant runs it. Actually, he's married to my mother. He needed a green card when he found her wandering homeless on the street. She needed someone to put her up and pay her rent. They don't sleep together, she told me. It's an honorable arrangement. I'm glad someone is taking care of her. I sure can't. I walk dogs for a living.

I drink my coffee and eat my pie. There is no one else in the diner. Only the waitress, whom I mentally molest even as I smile at her politely.

She has no idea what a fiend I really am, beneath the carefully fabricated façade.

The waitress is pretty, at least with lots of makeup, and she has a nice figure and seems as sad and lonely and desperate as I am. Neither of us is in a position to be picky. But I have no time to seduce a stranger right now. Mother is expecting me. I finish my food and pay my check.

Back in her apartment, she is sitting on the sofa, rocking back and forth, humming the tune "Those Were the Days." She does that a lot. It's a continuous loop permanently engrained in her damaged brain. Repetition is one of her coping mechanisms. It's like she's trying to convince herself of something only she understands.

I walk over and kiss her on her cold, clammy forehead, breaking her trance. She does not kiss me back. She stands up without making eye contact, says "Good night" in a perfunctory manner, then walks right past me. She doesn't know how to display affection or any emotion, really. It's just not in her, not anymore, not after a lifetime of relentless pain. Her heart is empty, her soul is broken. She is the walking dead. I understand.

I am constantly haunted by this biological and spiritual connection. It's nobody's fault. Just how the dice roll sometimes.

I feel very numb inside myself, like my soul (if I have one) was shot with Novocain. I suppose I should feel either some sort of cathartic release of joy and self-discovery or a deeply disturbing, melancholic sense of tragic waste. I mean I've just met a beautiful woman that carried me around in her gut, purposely or not, for nine months and then went through the physical agony of spewing me forth into this enigmatic carnival of beauty and horror. When I first embrace her, I experience a vaguely erotic sensation of physical consummation. I am flesh of her flesh, blood of her blood, even part of her accursed soul.

I lay on the couch for a while, staring at the ceiling. I am thinking about fucking that waitress back at the diner. I imagine unhooking her bra and emancipating her large breasts, which must smell of sweat and cheap perfume and greasy kitchen odors. In my mind I am smothering my face between them, suffocating. I was never breast fed, so I am obsessed with tits. Or so I tell myself. Eventually I doze off.

Sometimes I don't dream at all. It's just all black. That scares me, because it makes me think of death. My own death, that is. So now I've learned to force myself to dream. It's my only escape from my waking world, which is never one of my choosing.

I open my eyes and look at the clock on the wall. I can't make out the time. It's too dark and my eyesight is not that sharp anyway. But I do notice the crimson tip of a cigarette, glowing like the eye of a beast in a cave. My mother is just standing in the hallway, silhouetted in the darkness, staring at me silently. It freezes my heart like a sharp knock on the door in the middle of the night.

I pretend not to notice. I close my eyes and wish everything would go away.

When I open them again, she is gone. But I am still here.

The next morning I hide the kitchen knives.

Rain in the Night

I lean back on the bed as she pulls her blouse over her head and unhooks her bra. Free from their harness, her large breasts are still firm and upright, and appear whiter and smoother in the shadowy light of the room. Then she puts one high-heeled shoe on the bed as she unzips the side of her skirt, which she then removes with a wriggle, both feet back on the ground, her bare breasts swaying slightly as she stoops. Her skirt falls around her ankles as she kicks it away. Her high-heeled shoes are still on as she unfastens her garter and, once again putting a foot on the edge of my bed, begins sliding off her fishnet stockings, first one, then the other. She only slides them far enough down so that she doesn't have to remove her shoes. I like her shoes. She knows that, which is why she puts them back on after she sits down on the bed and slowly slips her stockings off her red-toenailed feet. I can smell her perfume from where I lie against two pillows and the headboard. The smoke from her cigarette causes a slight haze as it burns in an ashtray on the dresser. I don't like it when she smokes, but I make her nervous, and when she is nervous, she just has to light one up. Especially before sex. It relaxes her, she says, gets her in the mood.

Someone in the room across the alley is playing Chicago blues at peak volume, probably to drown out the street noise. We are in the International District of Seattle on a cool, cloudy night, and some adventurous tourists are still out and about. The residential hotel we occupy is on King Street. The room is cheap, but the sex is not.

I'd just blown a bundle on drinks and dim sum for the near-naked nymph nuzzling against my chest, kissing my neck and nipples as she strokes the inside of my thighs and massages my dripping wet genitalia, making it gush. Her touch makes me close my eyes and suck in my breath. I pet her smooth white shoulders and play with her breasts as she starts a trail of moist kisses leading from my throat and down my chest to my quivering groin.

I arch backwards as she caresses my sensitive parts with her warm tongue, then I lean forward and open my eyes to watch.

I let her hand wander freely over her own voluptuousness as she licks my sensitive parts gingerly, then hungrily. Just before I climax, I tap her head as a signal to stop, then I tenderly pull her up the length of my body and draw her into my arms. She is careful not to poke me with her high heels, which I keep glancing at deliriously. The sensation of her ample breasts against my chest gives me a rush of relief and pleasure. We kiss each other passionately, exploring each other's faces with our mouths as we roll around the creaky bed in a hot, sweaty embrace that steadily progresses from delicate caressing to frenzied wrestling.

She moves me around behind her as she leans on her arms and knees for me to mount her body from the rear. I find her vagina with my fingers and put two of them in as I rub her clitoris with my other hand. She moans and shakes from involuntary spasms of delight as I continue to manipulate her.

I reach around and feel her nipples grow hard as I find her rhythm and rock with it. I stop pleasuring her when she is just about to cum. She whispers a cuss word, then quickly rolls over on her back with her legs in the air. Her eyes are heavy-lidded with passion and her lips are swollen from kissing. I suck on her heaving breasts and drool on her stomach, then her loins and legs. As my tongue reaches her warm, wet hole, her hips buck forward and her thighs enclose my face. I eat her for what seems hours, maybe days. Outside I can hear rain along with the blues across the alley.

The street noise has died down, or maybe I am just so consumed by the moment that all other world events have been drowned out, along with the past and future. I lick her feet, still with the high-heeled shoes on, which keep nudging my shoulders and scratching my upper back, sometimes my lower back and buttocks, as I lap away at her lusciousness.

Finally, just before her moaning escalates into a final crescendo of hysteria, I follow my tongue up the length of her torso, absorbing the salty perspiration of her body and feeling drugged by the scent of her heat.

As my body melds fully with hers, and I rub our sensitive parts together in a subtle, circular motion, she claws at my back and kicks off her high heels, which land on either side of the bed. Her legs are drawn tightly around my hips as I kiss her throat and suck her nipples. When she isn't clawing at my back, she's running her fingers through my hair, and her long red-tipped fingernails make my flesh tingle with excitement.

She kisses my ear as I ululate on top of her, faster and harder as her groans grow more ecstatic. The bed sways and creaks as the rain pours outside. The wetness of her sensuality makes me dizzy. I feel like we are on an old ship in a storm at sea, drowning happily.

We achieve orgasm at the same time.

I lie on top of her for a while, our heavy breathing almost in sync, our pubic hairs entangled, her fluids sticky on my flesh, and mine on hers.

She just lies back with her eyes closed, sighing, and then she sits up on the edge of the bed for a moment before rising to get her cigarettes from the dresser.

The room is dark now, since many of the neon lights have been shut off after the storm washes away the throngs below. Now there is only the glow of her cigarette in the dark, and the soft, soothing sound of rain in the night.

When I open my eyes, there isn't even the rain. Just silence and darkness. My old friends.

She is lying beside me, very still, covered in her own blood, the same blood that is on my hands.

I am still in the dream. I have to wake up now and go walk the dogs.

Dreams of a Dog Walker

I awake suddenly, sitting up, shaking, from the dream. I hear a train wail in the distant darkness. It is the dead of night, and the eerie vividness of the dream seems truer than life.

I feel the familiar emptiness. The train sounds like the personification of my yearning.

It is happening again. I am out in the woods in Magnuson Park near Lake Washington, walking a dog, when I notice four tornadoes coming at us from every direction. The dog howls with the winds, and the train. The sky is as white as a corpse. The leaves blow from the trees, and their branches are soon bare.

"Theme Romantique" by Michel Jarre is still playing in the air, as it always does when I walk the dogs around the lake. I never knew where the music is coming from, but it doesn't matter. I like it. It is soothing, especially in times like these, though the howling tornadoes are starting to drown it out.

I rush home with the dog to seek shelter. I put the dog inside my own house, since we don't have time to make it back to his. Or hers. The dog is a black Lab. I walk several black and golden Labs regularly, as well as every conceivable breed. The sexes of all my canine clients are undistinguishable to me. Genitalia are such an arbitrary form of distinction between individuals.

The tornadoes are close enough now to touch as I stand on the porch briefly before going inside and huddling with the dog.

My place is dimly lit and strangely cozy, just another sanctuary from just another late afternoon storm. I pace the room. There is suddenly a knock at the door. Reluctantly, I answer it.

It is my wife, from whom I've been separated for over a year, or so it seems. I have lost track of time, at least in my waking life. Only the dream makes sense to me anymore. I am no longer sure she even exists outside of my own mind. Maybe I was never married at all.

She reminds me of my mother, actually.

In any case, she wants to discuss a possible reconciliation. Nice timing, I say as I close the door on the tornadoes. We small talk briefly, the dog resting at our feet, and then abruptly she leans into my arms and kisses me. I feel loved.

She tells me about her own recurring dream. She is always standing on a cliff at midnight, looking out at the dark horizon and black ocean. As she describes it, I am transported with her to the scene of her dream.

When she tries to hurl herself into the wave-swept rocks below, I stop her. Normally I am not there to save her from herself. I tell her I am glad I am there to rescue her this time from her self-induced fate, which happens to her over and over, every night, until now.

It is then we see a stairway extending indefinitely into the opaque firmament. We step onto them and ascend, groping through the mists and taking special care not to slip and plunge into the voracious depths of the sea below.

We continue climbing until we come upon a tombstone that apparently floats in midair. We are suddenly inside a celestial cemetery. Reality can be so strange sometimes.

Then we see the name on the tombstone. It is hers. I haven't saved her, after all.

The shock of this discovery causes me to stumble and lose my footing. I try to grasp her hand, but it slips right through my fingers. She is disappearing right in front of me.

I have to get back to my apartment. The dog is waiting for me. It is my responsibility to take care of him. Or her.

The Darkness of Daylight

Gun-shy desperadoes hide in the shadows. I am not sure what that means. I just appreciate the sound of it. It's like music with cryptic lyrics. For me, it's all about the melody, not the words.

When I go out, in the dream, I wear a long black leather coat, leather boots, and sunglasses. And nothing else, nothing beneath the shiny dark facade. I always carry an umbrella, which I can use as a weapon or as a weather repellant. I am always ready to defend myself against whatever comes.

In my waking world, I feel naked, but I am not. I am just very vulnerable to forces beyond my control. We all are. But I am the only that realizes it, apparently.

The dog I am walking at this moment starts coughing, then vomits. He or she has eaten something that doesn't agree with him or her. I hope that's all it is, anyway. I stoop down and hug him. Or her.

After I stand back up, the dog looks up at me with a mixture of love and sadness. This is the distilled emotional core of all life. Only animals realize this. They contain the truth of this world, but cannot share it with us, because we do not speak their simple language. We remain oblivious to the obvious nature of the physical universe, convinced we are its rightful rulers.

Animals know otherwise. Nature herself is in charge. We are merely minions in Her creation, subject to Her whims. Earthquakes. Tornados. Hurricanes. Droughts. Floods. Disease.

But the dog and I understand each other. We communicate silently, just by looking into each other's eyes. I sense its secrets, even if I cannot fully grasp them.

I think the dog pities me. But he or she loves me too. Unconditionally. I feel the same way. Not about myself. About the dog, and all animals. I do not comprehend my own species. Humans are a mystery I have no desire to solve.

It's almost always cool and cloudy here in Seattle. That's why I live here. I can't remember where I lived before, if anywhere. I can't even remember where my apartment is sometimes. I just spend my days walking the dogs. I never see the faces of their owners, my clients. I have keys, and let myself in, just to retrieve the dogs. The clients leave cash on the counter next to the dog treats.

I never poke around their apartments. My clients trust me. And I trust them, even if I'm not sure who they are. They know who I am, though.

Not even I know that much.

Dog walking is my only source of income, at least in my waking world, where I lead a very humble, solitary life, except for my canine companions. I only truly thrive in my dreams. That's where I am never alone. And there, I make my money by simply stealing it. I mug pedestrians when it's dark, as it always is, but mostly I just rip off my johns after I kill them.

Sometimes when I am walking a dog around the lake, while awake, I will wind up in the town where I grew up, or in another city, perhaps one I lived in before moving to Seattle. I can never be sure. I have no control over it. But at least I have the ability to fly. When I am anywhere where I feel uncomfortable, I pick up the dog and return to the lake.

Often we find ourselves in strange places that are seemingly mish-mashes of several somewhat familiar yet disturbingly surreal shadows of actual places I must've been before. They have certain streets and buildings and other landmarks of places from my distant past, but when combined in this fashion, they take on a distorted and distinctive collective ambience. And they are always the same, every time I return, however involuntarily. I never even know how I get there. Only that I want to leave. At least, after visiting for a brief time. As long as I have a dog with me, I feel safe.

I wish I could fly in my dreams. Sometimes I need to get away very quickly after committing one of my crimes against humanity, my sins against nature. Even though I know it's a dream and I can act accordingly with complete impunity, I always feel paranoid, being pursued by unseen forces that are constantly watching me. That is why I always do things in total secrecy, hiding my behavior from everyone else that shares my dream world, even though I know they are only phantoms.

But they don't know. I can tell by the way they react to me sometimes. Like it's all real.

Only I know the truth of this dream world. Like a dog in the real world.

I never hurt animals, even in the dream. They are such innocent creatures. Unlike humans. But I never hurt those types of beings in my waking world, either. At least not on purpose. Only in the dream, where they deserve it most. Where I can get away with it. Where it doesn't matter.

For some reason, I hardly ever see any of my kind when I'm awake. I don't miss them.

The Inner Limits

I slit his throat as he's going down on me, just as I cum all over his face and throat, so his blood combines with my fluids as they drip down his muscular chest, his throat gurgling with the overdose of fatal fluids. He looks at me with shock and sadness, as if he didn't see this coming. As it were. But it was my plan all along. He disgusts me.

I have no problem finding victims in my dream. I must be extremely attractive there. Hard to tell, because every time I look in the mirror, it tells a different story. My own identity is elusive to me. I can only imagine how others see me. But when they do see me, up close and personal, it isn't for long, and I don't give them much of a chance to make any memories. Not any that they'll have time to remember, anyway.

Thunder booms in the dark sky outside as he drops dead and continues dripping his essence, and mine, all over the hardwood floor, where it seeps into the cracks and between the boards, soaked up quickly, blending with the gallons of dried bodily fluids already evaporated into faded stains.

I don't pay rent for this room. I fuck the manager on a regular basis in exchange for my keep. That's why I haven't killed him yet. But someday I will, when I'm tired of living here. I won't let him know ahead of time. It will be a surprise.

Earlier tonight, before this dead man and I went up to my hotel room in the International District, we had gone down to Belltown and had dinner. I ate my usual vegetarian meal. He ordered a steak, and seemed to really relish it, licking his chops as he consumed the innocent flesh of the slaughtered cow.

That's when I knew I had to kill him. That kind of cruelty to animals cannot be tolerated. Not by me. Not in the dream, at least. In my waking world, humans literally get away with murder. Not here, never in the dream. This is my world. Not even Nature herself has any jurisdiction.

He keeps staring at me lustfully as we eat and chat in a restaurant facing Puget Sound, entranced by my apparent beauty, hypnotized by my breasts, judging by the trajectory of his gaze. I don't feel self-conscious, though. In the dream, I am all-powerful, so I'm accustomed to being in complete control, unlike in my waking life, where I pick up puppy poop for a living. I'm happy to serve the dogs, though. I am even subservient to humankind when I'm awake.

But not now. I own them. I am free to do anything I want with them. What does it matter? They're not real, anyway. They just don't know it. People in your dreams never know they're simply phantoms of your subconscious imagination. That's the beauty of it.

In my waking life, I never hurt anyone. I can't. I don't possess the capability to inflict harm on any sentient being. I am afflicted with deep empathy, even for my own species, though they fundamentally repulse me.

I do enjoy sex with them, though. That's basically all they're good for. In the dream, I can fuck whomever I please, whenever I want, then dispose of the body once I'm finished with it. It's a perfect world. If only it weren't a dream.

It feels so real, though. Even more real than my waking life. But then that's probably because I spend a lot more time in the dream, on purpose. I sleep as often as possible when not walking dogs, just so I can enjoy the dream, which, unlike my waking life, is completely different every time I'm there. It's so exciting, so invigorating. But I am very lonely in the dream, despite all the erotic encounters. I miss my friends, the dogs. The cats. The rabbits. All of the animals I watch for other people. I should just get some of my own. But that's too much responsibility. I need my own private time and space to indulge in my nocturnal fantasies. It's my soul's single release from this hell called Life. At least until I die.

But I am afraid of dying, because then I would never be in the dream. Unless, of course, the dream is the true reality, and my soul lives there for eternity. But then no more dog walking. Not a fair trade-off. I need both parallel planes to remain happy. Or at least sane. Relatively, that is. It's a matter of balance.

Anyway, after I fuck then kill this hunk of ephemeral human flesh, I chop him up and put him in the suitcase, then drive to Whidbey Island, where I bury the pieces in my own private graveyard. It's very peaceful there. In fact, burying the body parts is one of my favorite parts of the dream, because I love the serenity of the remote scenery.

I know, I could just toss the body out the window into the alley, and who would care? It's only make-believe, anyway. But in my dream, I've discovered there are certain rules of engagement with the other inhabitants, despite their lack of corporeal substance. It's like a game, really. And I'm always the winner, as long as I play by the rules, which I obviously invented, often making them up as I go. That means I can also break them any time I please. But I don't. I don't want to disturb the continuity of the ongoing narrative, which consistently surprises and delights me. My dream is my refuge. I need for it to remain as perfect as possible.

Otherwise I might go insane.

A Face Without Eyes

I can hear Maurice Jarre's "Theme Romantique" as I walk the dog, as usual. I'm not sure of its source at the moment, but it's originally from my favorite movie, *Eyes Without a Face*. It's the only movie I ever watch now, mainly because I love the ending, when the disfigured girl, wearing her mask, releases all of the animals from captivity as this music plays.

When I watch this movie in my waking life, I only perceive bits and pieces, and sometimes it seems like it's intermingling with my reality, so I can't tell the difference anymore. The screen of my television has no borders. It all blends together like bodily fluids.

Except in the dream, I have nobody.

This movie is in French, and my waking life is not. But it's also in black and white, like my dream. The vivid colors of my waking world exist in stark contract to the bleak chiaroscuro of my nocturnal world. I appreciate the colors of the trees, the lake, the dogs. But in my dream, everything is in various shades of gray, even the bodily fluids. The blood looks black to me. That's all right. It reminds me that it's not real, even though the sensations I am experiencing feel even truer than in my other world, the one that is supposedly the only one, at least for the rest of humanity.

That is why I kill them off, one by one, in the dream. It's my greatest pleasure, besides walking the dogs. If only I could merge the two worlds into one, I'd be in paradise. As it is, I'll settle for the dual existence in two different worlds. It's better than total oblivion, which is my ultimate fate, unless I have a spirit. But sometimes I think only animals have spirits. Humans just don't seem worthy of eternity.

The animals I see in the dream are very friendly, and I always stop to hug them, if their owners permit the proximity. But I know they're not real, the animals, so it makes sad. I don't want to get attached, only to have them suddenly disappear, like they never existed. It's hard enough in my waking life. Animals don't live nearly long enough. It's not fair. Their brief life spans are one of the great tragedies of the waking world. At least in my dreams, I know they're immortal. But unfortunately unreal. Fantasy is the only thing that endures, at least in the minds of future generations. I wish I could leave something of myself behind in the "real" world, besides dog shit. But I don't even leave that. I always pick it up and place it in the trashcan, as required, though I'd prefer to leave it out to fertilize the grass.

That's how we all wind up, ultimately – as either trash or fertilizer, or both. I can only hope my spirit lives on inside the dream, forever.

Animals leave no legacy, though. Their only gift to the world is love, and it never lasts. In return, they are hunted, murdered, and devoured. I wish I could punish humans in my waking life, but maybe it's for the best that my revenge is unleashed in the dream, where I can strike without fear of punishment or incarceration. My conscience wouldn't allow me to kill people in the waking world, anyway. Like I said, I could never inflict pain on a real person. Only the phantoms in my dream.

My wet dream, I should say. It is drenched in bodily fluids. The blood, semen and vaginal juices are like a river running through my consciousness. Without this liquid sustenance, I'd dry up and wither away in the desert of my loneliness.

Does that sound poetic? Or just pathetic?

I can't hear you or see you. But I know you are there, watching, and judging me. I am immune to your hypocritical, self-righteously moral superiority. You can't touch me in my dream, only in my waking life.

But you don't know where I am, because I don't either. You will never find me. I will never find myself. I know, because I stopped looking long ago.

Chiaroscuro

I first realize that my dream world is in fact only a dream when I notice everything is in black and white, like an old movie. Only my waking world is in color. I can't remember if my dreams were always colorless, or if my waking world was always colorful. But ever since I made that distinction, I've behaved accordingly.

I rub my moist genitals all over her curvaceous body, mixing our fluids, absorbing her essence. I cum again as I lick the blood from her breasts, neck, and torso. Then I tongue her dead mouth with her own gore. And cum again.

I wonder why I never wake up wet, since I achieve orgasm so often in my dreams. I never have sex while awake. I don't need to. My nocturnal journeys more than satisfy my cravings for human flesh, however unreal it actually is. That's why I can consume so much of it, though. It is healthier than eating soy substitutes that only taste like meat. Or at least it's more carnally satisfying.

I first begin eating my victims after my fiftieth or so kill, by my count, though it's all a bit fuzzy in my mind, since after all, none of it is actually happening. Before that decision I am content merely fucking and killing them, then disposing of their bodies, as I've explained. But after witnessing the consumption of so much innocent animal flesh in my waking world, the memory of that actually carries over to my subconscious, and my lust for revenge equals my taste for sensuality.

At first I feel like a hypocrite, since after all, in my waking life I am a strict vegan. I am very healthy, in fact. I have never once smoked, drunk alcohol, or taken drugs in my entire life. My sense of self-preservation won't allow me to indulge in such self-destructive vices. Plus I am responsible for my canine, feline and other animal clients. They count on me to be there for them. So I can't die. Ever, if I can help it. Even though they keep dying, and it devastates me each time.

However, in the dream, I revel in the deaths of humans, which I cause myself. Eating their flesh and organs seems like a natural progression, especially since none of it is actually happening, anyway.

And yet, the sensations, both of sex and killing, as well as the consumption of fresh human corpses, are so palpable that I'd swear they are actually happening. But if they are, I'm sure I would've been caught by now.

I'm careful anyway, because for all I know, ultimate justice exists in my private dream universe, just like it does in my corporeal alternate reality, where authority is actually imposed on our sense of morality. But in the dream, I am the ultimate authority, as far as I know. I don't risk exposure of my sins, though. Just in case I am wrong.

Anyway, the very first piece of human meat I devour while the victim is still alive. I am going down on this guy and suddenly have the urge to just bite his dick off. So I do. He screams and bleeds, screams and bleeds, until I slice his throat with his own razor. Then I drink his blood. It tastes sweet, at least in the dream, while the flesh is salty. I think I read this fact somewhere while awake, so the suggestion seeps into my subconscious. That's how I can experience these sensations while asleep, inside my own head, and enjoy them as if they are real.

It's then that I decide I am actually a vampire in my dream. Except when I am a werewolf. In fact, I am a vampire that sometimes turns into a werewolf, on a whim. I can be whatever I choose to be within that world, unlike the other one, where I'm just a dog walker.

I love the freedom of the dream! I'm totally emancipated to do things I could never do in my waking world. Except for flying, that is. For some reason I can only fly when I'm awake. I wonder why no one ever sees me, except for the dogs. And they'll never tell. You can trust them with all your secrets.

Sometimes when I look into an animal's eyes, it seems they're trying to tell me something. But because I'm a stupid human, I can't understand what they're trying to say. It could be the secret of the universe, encompassing both of my worlds. Or the answer to what happens to us when we die, or rather, when our physical bodies expire. Do we have spirits that live on? And will mine exist eternally within the confines of my dream?

I don't know. I can't understand what they're trying to tell me, beyond the fact they love me, and understand I love them too. I am avenging the deaths of their brothers and sisters, but only in the dream. I could never get away with it in my actual life. So I don't even try.

There is one person in my dream that continues to elude me. Sometimes I see her, in a crowd, but when I get close, she's gone. She is quite beautiful. In fact, she reminds me of my mother when she is young. Sometimes I wonder if that is who it actually is, since in a dream, time and death are meaningless. But I can't say for sure until I actually catch up with her. Meantime, she's simply haunting me.

I can even see her when I'm awake sometimes, but that's only if I close my eyes. I can't see her when they're open. Only when my mind is open, at night.

Daylight blinds me to my own truth.

Neurotica

It's strange how in my waking life, I am celibate and only watch pornography, but in my dream, I act out all of my most perverse fantasies, and then dismember and dispose of my various partners. Or rather, my playthings.

When not walking dogs, I either watch *Eyes without a Face*, or X-rated videos. My dreams seem to be a combination of both, which makes sense. I mean, as much sense as I can make of anything.

Sometimes I imagine the movie as being X-rated, even though it's old (though it is French). I envision all sorts of erotic scenarios for the characters. Somehow it's not as crass in black-and-white. It's rather beautiful, in fact. Just like my dream.

Blood has no color in my dream. It's just black. Unless you consider black to be a color. Every now and then, someone's eyes will flash red as I kill them. Or blue or green when they achieve orgasm. And sometimes their cum is red, too. Just like their eyes, before the light in them goes out.

Other times, the moon above, which is always full, turns red. And sometimes the ocean is blue and green. The cityscape is always gray, though, in varying shades. The people are gray too, like zombies. Like shadows.

It all feels so real. Only my waking life feels unreal. Except for the dogs.

This one woman is going down on me, and when she lifts her face, it is covered in red fluids. My fluids. It freaks me out. I immediately sit up and snap her neck. Then I pleasure myself on her corpse, rubbing my scarlet fluids all over her warm flesh, before it grows cold. It doesn't matter. She isn't actually dead, since she was never actually alive. Except in my mind.

Another time this guy breaks his fingers in my ass. He screams. I laugh and laugh. Then I pick up the lamp and bash his skull till it explodes.

I love being in control of my own world. It's the only way to live. Even if it's all a dream.

I tell a psychiatrist this once. This is before I realize the psychiatrist is just another inhabitant of my dream, and I kill her after raping her. Or maybe it is a man. I don't remember. Their sex makes no difference. Nothing does. They're just phantoms with bloody orifices. They do not actually exist.

Sometimes I wonder if I exist, outside of the dream, that is. I hope so. I don't want the dogs to be alone, ever. I understand the pain of loneliness. They don't deserve to suffer like that. People do.

I miss the colors of autumn in my dream. That is the only downside of dying then being trapped there forever.

Colors are the best thing about my waking life, besides the dogs. I don't need sex when I'm awake. Though I do masturbate to the pornographic images on my screen, and sometimes, in my mind, remembering my many erotic experiences in the dream, which are so fantastic, so free.

I dare not attempt any of these things in my waking life. I would eventually get caught, then imprisoned, probably executed for these horrible crimes against humanity. I could never abandon the dogs like that. They need me. And I need them. Otherwise, my waking life has no purpose.

Thank God I have the dream. It is the safe haven for my darkest desires.

I don't know how anyone else survives without their own dreams.

Unless both worlds are dreams. In that case, I am truly alone in the universe.

And that is fine with me. As long as the animals are real.

Motherfucker

Someone once told me people only remember what they want to remember. But I can't remember who told me that.

We're on the subway, presumably under Manhattan, going back to Brooklyn. I am very small, but I can understand my mother's words as she rants and raves. She is pacing up and down the train, yelling at everyone, or anyone that will pay attention, which is no one. They all cower behind their magazines and newspapers, trying their best to ignore her. I can't. I'm trapped with her. In fact, I'm trapped *within* her. I'm inside of her womb. Ring side seat to her inner turmoil.

She says I ruined her life. Meaning me, her unborn child. Her career as an actress will never happen now, thanks to this unplanned pregnancy. My father could be any number of men, but it doesn't matter. She does not want me, but is afraid to abort me, because she was raised to believe that is a sin. As opposed to hating your own offspring and blaming them for all your misfortune. That's just fine.

But she was rejected too. Despite her worldly advantages, like comfort and beauty. She was rejected by the whole world. By Life itself. Or so she believes. Her illness makes her an instant social pariah, overwhelming her former attributes, which are no compensation, either for her or anyone else. So she takes affection wherever she can get it, from whoever will give it to her, for whatever selfish reason.

I am inside of her as the penises of many strangers poke around her vagina, finally splashing me with their seedless sperm. I feel her buck as she orgasms, then I feel her body racked with sobs.

Then suddenly one of them, one of those men, I think, perhaps even my own father, is on top of me, fucking me furiously. The transition is very abrupt, skipping decades ahead in time and space, leaving me disoriented and submissive to the lurid circumstances. I feel him penetrate me as he holds down my wrists and grinds into my loins, suckling my breasts, slobbering on my face and neck as he cums, again and again, or so it seems. I cum as well. I can't help it. It is very exciting.

I look into his face as he grimaces with pleasure. He is sweaty and hideous. I normally choose attractive partners, so his ugliness is jarring and deeply disturbing, and quite humiliating. I feel his hard muscles, on his arms and chest, but also the smaller bumps and humps all over his back and shoulders and neck. He is extremely huge, inhumanly so, and severely deformed. His massive, throbbing member is like a mutated slab of raw meat, thrusting over and over, viciously violating my body and soul. I feel myself crack open and bleed profusely onto the bed sheets, already sticky with his gallons of semen spilling out of us both. I cannot get him off of me. He cannot get enough of me. He is devouring me.

It's then I notice his horns. On his head. And the fangs in his gaping mouth, biting my throat and nipples, making them drip blood all over my torso, blood that he swallows, as I swallow the semen from his cock. And then there is his long, prehensile forked tongue, licking me all over, from head to toe, slurping up our fluids.

And his eyes, his red eyes, glowing like neon. And his leathery flesh is green, like a lizard. His are the only colors I can see. The rest is black, all black, except for my own pale white flesh. And except for the fluids, which are red. Otherwise, we are fucking in a cold void, swirling around, intimately entwined, engulfed by shadows and mist, or perhaps it's smoke, generated by our heat.

So that explains it. He is not human after all. He is a demon, and he is raping me so hard I can't even scream except with pleasure, because I am overwhelmed by his lust, consumed by his passion, filled with his fluids, which burn inside of me as he leers and drools and cums, again and again, and I cum with him, in delirious tandem, if also in utter terror.

He turns me over and pushes his enormous cock into my ass, and pushes it so far inside of me I can feel his semen flooding the back of my throat as he cums. Blood is gushing out of me again, along with his semen, dripping down my thighs and onto the bed, which is so sopping wet it's trickling onto the slippery floor, staining the boards anew. I have no power at all to stop this. I am not even sure I want to. Maybe I deserve this. But that's not the point.

There is thunder and lightning too, emanating from somewhere, but maybe I'm just imagining that part. It's hard to tell now.

This has never happened before. I am losing control over my own dream. I must be dying.

Dog's Will

It is the day after this dream, which is my first true nightmare, that one of my canine clients starts talking to me, in human language. I think it's English, but I'm not sure. He is an old dog. He tells me he is dying from cancer, slowly and then quickly, but his owners don't know it yet. They think he is perfectly healthy, because he hides his pain, out of deference to their inevitable grief. This is how animals are. They are so much better than humans.

The old dog is only sharing this private information with me because he knows how devastated I will be when the time comes, very soon. He understands that unlike his owners, I have no one else in my life, besides my other clients. No humans to offer me comfort. His tells me his eyes are already fading as we watch the ducks swimming in the lake. I hug his neck and bury my face into his fur, and weep. He licks away my tears and tells me he will see me again. In my dream.

This is the only time this has ever happened to me. I swear.

Waves

When I visit her in Brooklyn, Mother tells me she feels electricity shooting through her head. She says no one but me believes her. And I am lying to her when I say I do.

As she tells me this, she is staring into space as if in a manic trance, deciphering strange telepathic messages that randomly shoot through her skull like lightning across stormy waters.

She hums to herself often, sometimes a popular old tune, like "Those Were the Days," or sometimes "Greensleeves" or "Love Is Blue," songs from her youth. But mostly I just hear soft sounds emanating from a place deep inside her tortured consciousness. They sound like small, feeble cries for help, muted and weakened by the time they work their way through the mire of her mind and out into the reality consuming her pathetic existence with parasitic determination.

She continues to live because she fears the only other alternative. To this, I can relate.

Sometimes I have a vision of my mother when she is young and beautiful and full of hope, before the madness destroys her life and dreams. It is a repressed memory that floats in my brain like a mist; it would dissipate if touched. We are together in a sparsely furnished room somewhere. She is standing in a darkened doorway, bathed in light from an outside source, possibly the setting sun, making her shoulder length hair glow inside a halo. The shadows of twilight make our bleak little room vibrate with mystery. She is close enough to see, but too far away to touch, because I can't move from the bed. The mood of melancholia pervading the short distance between us makes me long for her like an intangible illusion in a wasteland. I freeze this indeterminate moment in time, like a painting of dimensional reality, or a scene from a movie too romantic for truth.

Love's agony can destroy you, but love's bliss can liberate you.

Revolutions

It's not that I spend all of my time thinking about what might've been. It's more like I waste all of my time trying not to.

I was planning to be a famous actor. Then a famous writer. I wanted to rebel against my own fate.

Neither worked out. I am just a dog walker. Fate wins, as always.

Otherwise, I pretend to be something I'm not, or rather, someone I don't want to be. My life is happening against my will. Except in the dream.

I love walking dogs. But I can't say it gives me a true feeling of fulfillment. Just a sense of purpose. Those are not necessarily the same things.

I feel a sense of peaceful calm when I am walking the dogs around the lake or through the quiet woods. In the dream, it is all carnal chaos and relentless horror. But at least I am in charge there. It is my private movie, my internal stage.

Outside the dream, I often feel like a fugitive on the run who suffers from amnesia and so can't remember what my crime is and why I'm being hunted and persecuted. Maybe my crime is non-conformity. I just feel too much, and think too much for my own good.

There's no respect for passion anymore, because of society's selfish apathy. Nobody cares if nobody else cares about anything. Play the game, or don't. If you win, you're celebrated for a few minutes, then forgotten. If you lose, tough luck. The next revolution will arise from ennui, not passion.

I once yearned to be rich and famous so I could justify not only my existence, but Mother's. I've given up on those youthful ambitions, just as she surrendered hers to forces too powerful to battle. I think about what might've been as I walk the dogs around the lake, over and over and over. I can't help it.

I know she thinks about what might've been too, wherever she is. I know she thinks about me. I know she thinks about me, thinking about her. That's my only consolation. Our psychic link across all boundaries.

It is also what saddens and horrifies me. I can't escape this loop. I can only transfer it to the dream, my secret realm of manifest destiny.

Infanticide

I am told that when I was only a baby, my mother flew into a rage and bounced me against a wall. That's when I was taken away from her, and raised in foster homes. Like an orphaned dog.

I don't know if that's true, because I can't remember it. I can certainly imagine it, though. Does that make it less real?

Mother denies it, but that doesn't mean it's not true. Denial of the truth is her specialty. It's part of the human condition, in fact. It's how we survive as a species. Ignoring the obvious, pretending our lives are not finite, that some glorious reward for enduring this nightmare awaits us in the hereafter.

Maybe she should've strangled me in my crib. Or better yet, never had me at all. Then all the people I've killed would still be alive, if only in a dream I was never alive to invent.

Would they even know the difference? Would I?

This is my point. Existence is not only ephemeral; it's relative to our consciousness. Killing a baby might very well be an act of mercy.

Too late now. Here I am, passing on the pain. An endless cycle that can only end when I die.

But many others will take my place. I am expendable.

So are you.

Dream Noir

Back in the dream, I begin noticing that all of the people are now monsters. Not just demons. Rotting corpses, my former lovers, are now zombies wandering the streets. Some are more like vampires. All sorts of monstrosities. I have no choice. I must fuck them all again. Or let them fuck me. There is nothing else to do here now, anyway. Nothing else gives me any pleasure. I am increasingly unhappy in the dream, because I no longer feel it is my world. I belong to it now. Just like in my waking life. There is no escape, except for death. But death terrifies me. My only hope is my greatest fear.

Meantime, I continue my regular nocturnal routine. I am compelled to do so, by forces greater than I. This is my new dream. I have no choice.

My first night in the revised, rebooted version of the dream: One of the many zombies approaches me in a bar as I am drinking a martini, listening to the jazz quartet on stage. Ironically, I never drink alcohol in my waking life, because I need to remain lucid and alert for my dog walking. I never even listen to any music in my waking life, other than "Theme Romantique," but that's not on purpose. It's just there, like ambient sound, all of the time. But here, in the dream, all the music is jazz. Or a kind of jazz. It is sometimes shrill and dissonant, not melodic. Like screaming saxophones. In fact, it all sounds exactly the same. At least to me. But then I've never been much of a connoisseur.

The zombie is a male, I think. But since all flesh rots, even in the dream, sex is irrelevant. I let him take me to his hotel room. He rips off my clothes then tears into my flesh. He is eating me alive.

But no matter how much of my flesh he chews and swallows, I still have more. I can see part of his skull, brain, guts and skeleton. One eye falls out inside of me as he is going down on me. I suck his cock and it breaks off in my mouth, his cum, or rather his pus, running down the sides of my mouth, down my throat, onto my breasts. I spit it out. He just puts it back on and then fucks me up the ass till he cums pus all over my internal organs. We are as one now.

This happens again and again. I fuck zombies, demons, vampires. They fuck me back, even harder. It is a cannibalistic orgy of flesh and fluids. And I cannot be sated, no matter how many strange monsters have their way with me. And neither can they.

I don't even kill them anymore. I just fuck them, then move on to the next one. They're already dead, anyway.

The Thing That Ate Me

I don't even know what It is. It is carrying me into the dark, dirty little room, where It lays me down and has Its way with me, for hours, maybe days. I start worrying about the dogs in my waking life. But I cannot break away. Literally. It chains me to the rickety bed, and then eats and fucks me continuously. It is ape-like in appearance, but its misshapen body is only partly covered in patches of course fur. Its breath is foul, Its teeth jagged and crooked. Even Its cum stinks. But It showers me, fills me, and I gladly bathe in Its liquid filth.

When I wake up, the dog is beside me, his head on my lap. We are sitting on the shore of Lake Washington, as usual. I must have dozed off.

So did he. He is dead.

When I return to the dream, I look for him, as he promised. But he is not there.

Sustenance

In what passes as the real world, people are addicted to the illusion of happiness. They are so willfully and blindly complacent, it makes me physically ill. Watching them laughing in the deceptive death rays of the oppressive sun at their little barbecues, making stupid jokes as they callously devour burnt animal flesh, is the height of hypocrisy to me. Their materialism also bores and offends me. They have no respect for the pure spirits of the sweet beasts whose flesh they gleefully violate. Their priorities are all mixed up.

Of course, this world I'm describing is one I only know from television shows and commercials. I have never experienced it first hand, since as I recall, I was raised by wolves that lived in caves equipped with electricity. But I have witnessed this luxurious lifestyle, up close and personal. In restaurants and at picnics by the lake. People eating dead animals and arguing politics, self-righteous and indignant, denouncing man's inhumanity to man, assuming moral superiority and dominion over the Earth, even as they slaughter, butcher and consume its most innocent inhabitants.

I know from an early age I would have to even the score. But I can't do it while awake. Only in my dream. That is where true justice can be claimed. At least an imaginary facsimile of it, anyway. People don't really die in my dream. Only in my waking life.

And so do dogs, and all animals. Just seeing a dead bird or squirrel by the road makes me unbearably depressed. My misery is compounded by my loneliness. If all the animals die out, I will truly be all alone, trapped in a harsh world of heartless humans I am not free to kill.

But then they will soon die of starvation, unless they all become vegetarians. Maybe they'll resort to cannibalism. Like zombies. That is my fantasy.

And as usual, my fantasy only lives in my dream, where the zombies and monsters have taken over the Earth, killing and eating each other and the remaining humans in an endless, pointless battle assuring mutual destruction, as I frantically search amid the violent chaos for the dead dog. But soon the animals shall inherit the Earth, anyway. The one in my dream, that is.

This is when I notice I am being followed.

Shadows in the Fog

Sometimes I feel like a detective trying to solve the mystery of my own existence. I'm perpetually in pursuit of a shadow in the fog enshrouding me. I don't know what the shadow is, which is why I'm so determined to apprehend and interrogate it. It could be something tangible, like success, or ethereal, like love.

Maybe it's Mother.

But I think she's searching for the identity of the same shadow in different, more impenetrable mists. The shadow I'm tracking seems close at hand one second, and merely a peripheral illusion the next. Maybe it is only another diseased figment of my inexhaustible imagination. But my instincts tell me otherwise. My heart whispers incessantly to my brain, and the conflict of the philosophies inherent in these struggles is the genesis of my neuroses.

I am a sex fiend. I admit and accept this fact. The 1934 film *Maniac* confirms my self-diagnosis, because I have all the same symptoms.

This becomes clear when I realize I am not following the shadow in the fog. It is following me.

It's like I'm on a missing persons case, and the missing person is me.

Floaters

I start getting eye floaters when I am still relatively young. I am old now, at least in my waking life. But the eye floaters are startling and scary when they first begin, since they adversely affect my vision. I have already been suffering from migraines with aura since I was a child. The doctor says it is a nervous disorder, like epilepsy, possibly connected to my mother's illness, in which case it is hereditary. In any event, the migraines are diagnosed as being incurable, and not even really treatable. Just like schizophrenia (except for those over-rated anti-psychotic medications, which Mother says don't really work).

But my mother didn't bequeath me a physical or mental disorder, as far as I am concerned. She denies the medical diagnosis of schizophrenia anyway, referring to her condition as "acute awareness" instead. As far as we are concerned, our "nervous disorders" are the direct result of a much more elusive spiritual malady that exceeds the boundaries of medical science, passed on from generation to generation. So I decide at an early age to end this sad cycle by remaining celibate and meek in my waking life, but behaving like a homicidal whore in my dream.

The eye floaters normally afflict my peripheral vision, so it feels like there is always someone, or something, about to broadside me. It makes me rather paranoid, I must admit. The floaters themselves resemble dark cobwebs in the corners of my eyes, or pieces of dirt flittering in the corner of a film projected on a screen. I figure my cloudy brain is manifesting itself in my daily life. My waking life, that is.

But when I begin noticing them in my dream as well, that's when I realize something is very, very wrong.

I often think of the dog from my young adulthood, the one that saved me when I was wandering the streets as an orphan. I didn't adopt him (or her). It adopted me. I have felt very loyal and appreciative of its kind ever since. I owe them my life, for whatever that's worth. And I feel responsible for the death of my puppy, since it was under my care when it died.

Now, in the dream, I am suddenly running on all fours. I am the dead dog. Our spirits have merged. Maybe this is why so many of the monsters fuck me doggy style now. So I decide I am a werewolf. It is just a way to self-designate until I figure out what the hell is going on.

So I find it very troubling when I sense that I am under surveillance. By whom or by what, I cannot discern. But my animalistic senses are accurate. Someone is on to me. That means someone, or something, has infiltrated my dream, and disturbed the natural order of things.

Whenever I turn to see who it might be, they vanish. Eyes are on me everywhere, it seems. The paranoia from my waking world has finally seeped into my dream.

It reaches a new level when I read the headlines in the newspapers on the stands, which are blurry, since it is a dream, after all, but I can definitely make out the gist of what they're saying.

SEX KILLER STILL AT LARGE. And next to this headline is a drawing of the main suspect.

It looks just like me. Or at least someone that sometimes looks like me.

It's hard to tell with all these floaters obscuring my vision. I just wonder why I can discern the letters if it's only a dream, but that only proves how vivid they are.

At least to me. And I might be the only truly sentient being in the entire universe, on any plane of existence.

That is true loneliness.

Complex Messiah

I want to save all the animals in the world. They are so responsive to love. Unlike humans. People only respond to superficial sensations. Pain, pleasure. They are slaves to their darkest desires. Greed, lust, anger. They are selfish, insensitive, violent creatures. So I put them out of their misery. Or maybe it's just my misery.

But now I am concerned someone is trying to do the same to me. I might just let them. If they catch me.

Is it you?

Are you following me? I know you watch me, so you must be following me, too.

But you know I know you are there. We have an arrangement.

This is something, someone different. I am afraid.

The walls are bright and blinding, instigating a flurry of floaters. The fluorescent lights on the ceiling hurt my eyes. But I can't close them. I feel pressure on my temples, around my forehead. I feel pain in my brain. It is being drained of the dream.

I must fight it. The dream is all I live for. I hope I live there forever when I die. But first I must destroy my enemies there. Or else we will be trapped together for eternity.

But who will rescue and protect the animals in my waking world when I am gone?

For this reason I must survive as long as possible. For their sakes, not mine.

I look into their eyes, and say nothing. But they hear me. They know I can see them for who they really are, inside.

And they see me. The real me. That's how I know they are magical beings, intuitively superior to my kind, the false monarchs of the waking world.

Not even I can see me anymore.

Raison d'être

I exist in a perpetual state of confusion and apathy. The distractions that seem to bring joy to the simian phantoms inhabiting both my waking and dream worlds leave me cold and empty. Politics. Sports. Socializing. The Sun. I hate them all. And yet, they remain popular amongst the general population. This contributes to my sense of isolation. Except for the animals.

I don't understand the point of consciousness, much less sub-consciousness. Awareness of one's own pathetic existence and ephemeral surroundings is useless, because none of it ultimately matters. I am living proof of this. Or dying proof.

I lie awake in this sterile, harshly lit tomb and think of my life, whether memories or dreams, since both are the same in hindsight. You cannot touch them. This moment, the one you can feel and touch, is gone by the time you grasp it. Then this one. Then this one. Then this one. And so on.

That is why none of it matters. It all slips right through our fingers, which themselves will one day rot into the soil.

I wonder if animals realize this fact. Their lives are so short, and so simple. They thrive on the sustenance of very basic needs. I hope they are not aware of their own deaths, even when it arrives.

The dog that was sick has died. I no longer see him in my waking world. I am still looking for him in the dream.

Then I wonder: what do animals dream? Do my furry friends dream of me? Will I live on in their dreams after I am gone?

I read once that energy cannot be created nor destroyed. I don't believe that. But that doesn't mean it isn't true.

Lipoma

One day I feel a lump on my leg, and panic. I can't tell whether I am awake or dreaming. If I am dreaming, then it doesn't matter. If I am awake, then this could be the end. I might suddenly disappear, just like everyone else that eventually vanishes, like they were never here, leaving only traces of evidence in their wake. And even that eventually fades away.

The lump turns out to be nothing, a benign piece of fatty flesh just beneath the skin. My brain and heart are useless hunks of tissue, too. But they keep going anyway, like zombies. I operate on instinct. Like a dog.

I feel relieved that I don't have a malignant tumor. Except for the fact I still can't tell if I am awake or not. This is equally disturbing. I must proceed with caution. My responsibilities in each domain are so different. I cannot afford to confuse them.

I finally figure it out when I get a call to walk a dog. I only walk dogs in my waking world. I reach down with trembling trepidation and feel the lump. If it had been malignant, it would cripple and ultimately kill me. In both cases, I would be unable to walk the dogs anymore and fulfill my main function in the waking world.

For a fleeting moment, I feel grateful to be alive for the first time in my entire life. It is an oddly disorienting sensation.

As I walk the dogs, they lead me on the desolate but beauteous winding pathways, lined with lush, swaying trees and sparkling bodies of water. It is our journey together. I pray it lasts forever.

But it won't. Nothing does. This awareness makes me so sad. But maybe that's the lipoma talking. The lipoma inside my skull.

Canine Carnage

I have been training attack dogs to kill the humans in my dream. It doesn't require much encouragement. They share my innate disdain for my own species. They only pretend to be subservient and loyal in exchange for nourishment and shelter. But in their souls, they are like me. That is why I am the only human they truly trust. I whisper to them, and they not only understand me, but they heed my words.

Hunt. Kill. Feed. Fuck. Repeat.

I do not mean to denigrate the owners of the pets in my dream world. They are nice people, as far as people go. But I can see through the façade of existence, and they cannot. I feel sorry for them. But in my dream, my pity is expressed via vengeful violence.

I teach the dogs to kill the zombies. They rip and shred their decaying flesh, then spit it out, sometimes vomiting. I have trained them not to eat this putrid matter. They will remain pure, unadulterated by the consumption of corrupted carcasses.

Humans eat animals in both my worlds, without conscience, without mercy. I cannot let my dogs sink to their level.

My revenge is restricted to the slaughter. Their screaming satisfies my desire for justice.

I have stopped eating their flesh, too. I can no longer stomach it.

Now I am teaching the dogs to track the person or persons tracking me. It is only a matter of time now.

The spillage from my genitals soaks the sheets, blending with the blood. I begin chopping up the body. But I do not feed the pieces to the dogs standing guard outside the door.

I pack up the pieces, wrapped neatly in the bag, and dispose of them as I normally do, in the lake on the island. My dogs are always with me.

Then in the shadows I hear a sound, and detect movement. My trackers have found me.

The dogs bark and attack, but then stop short. There are two of them. One man, one woman. Both beautiful. Both nude. I cannot resist their seductive presence. It is overwhelming.

The three of us make love in the moonlight. The dogs watch over us.

I ask the strangers why they are following me.

They say they are my guardian angels. I say no, the dogs protect me.

They claim to be spirits assuming human form. That is why they are so physically perfect, because their corporeal forms are fabricated for fantasy. They bring me to sensual heights I have never experienced before, even in the dream.

After my last orgasm, I lay by the lake, blissfully unaware of my surroundings, engulfed in the ethereal mists of the surrounding forest. I feel free.

Then I look over and notice I am alone. The dogs are dead. Dismembered. The "spirits" are gone. Their erotic engagement was merely a cruelly contrived distraction. How human of them.

Then I look down and see the blood on my own hands. The guardian angels never existed. My dogs are my only protectors. And I killed them.

I weep uncontrollably, trying to wake up from this nightmare. But I cannot. I am trapped inside my own dream.

One

The light is blinding me. My floaters are clouding my vision. I begin to scream for help, or at least mercy.

Again, I do not know if I am awake or asleep, and this only adds to my terror. This is an increasingly frequent and alarming dilemma.

I feel strapped down. I cannot move. I feel my life essence draining from my veins. Then I realize my scream is silent. Or it's just falling on deaf ears.

I am alone. I call for my guardian angels, but they do not respond.

Because they were never there.

Maybe I'm not really here, either.

Then I feel a warm, familiar tongue licking my hand.

I open my eyes, and I am lying by the lake, with the dog that died. But he is not dead. Not anymore. He is alive, and giving me the love I need.

I hug and kiss him. He or she licks my face.

The sky is overcast. It begins to rain. We just sit there, watching the water from the sky blend with the water in the lake. It is all one element, one spirit, one consciousness.

The dog and I merge into a single being. Or so it seems as we rest our heads together, our minds as one, watching the rain fall into the lake.

Carnal Catharsis

I need to fuck. My vice is my voice. Otherwise, no one can hear me, and it's like I don't even exist.

My dogs help me find my next partner/victim. They are bloodhounds, tracing the scent of sex and death, the two most profound motivators of human behavior and the sources of our most profound moral conflicts.

I can't take the suffering of my victims seriously, because for one thing, it's not real, but also, their selfish complaints about social and economic injustice don't resonate in a world where most humans kill and consume innocent animal flesh. I don't care about their wages, or their laws, or their commerce, or even their civil rights. Their politics and religions are simply arbitrary rules with no resonance or relevance beyond our own ephemeral sphere, requiring blind, fruitless faith in an allegedly fair system of co-existence that is itself completely random, without any justice whatsoever. Their callous insensitivity to sentient beings other than their own species warrants nothing but disgust, because there's no excuse for such cruelty.

This also makes me very sad.

But in the dream, after I use these pathetic zombies and phantoms for sex, and kill them, I feel a sense of satisfaction. It is only momentary, both the pleasure and the catharsis.

Things are changing, though. I am on the run now, hiding, even in the dream. The authorities are on to me. I must play their game, or die.

I pick up a prostitute. We can no longer go to my hotel room in the International District, since it is under surveillance. We must fuck in the alley as the dogs stand guard. Even though they are only ghost dogs now.

It is very cold, but our bodies are warm. She is beautiful, too beautiful to be a cheap hooker. I lick and kiss and suck on her supple flesh. She licks and kisses and sucks on mine. We exchange fluids and cash. The rain washes away the evidence of our sin.

I can't kill her. Even though she isn't real. I am losing the urge. Or I am losing my mind. But how can you lose what you never had?

Fun in the Sun

I'm on the beach with my mother. I'm a little boy. The water is green, the sky is purple, the sands are white. Everything is in Technicolor. We're in Fort Lauderdale. She has moved here from New York, and seems happier, at least relatively, but maybe that's only because I'm here visiting her again. She wants me to move here, but I hate the sun.

The Arab is dead now, shot in the head during a late night robbery of his corner market. The perps were never caught, at least not by the police. Probably decaying at the bottom of the river. Mob justice. But none for the man that saved my mother from the streets, at least temporarily. She almost seems normal now, thanks partly to his support. He deserved better than such a violent, premature death.

But for now, my mother and I are enjoying this thing called Life for a change. Together. As it was always meant to be, at least in a perfect world. Of course, the only perfect world is the one we imagine.

The afternoon sun breaks through the clouds and burns my neck. The morning mists begin to fade away, but I can still feel their cool remnants wafting in off the Atlantic. The sudden warmth makes me uncomfortable. My skin begins to itch. I need to escape the brightness.

I run into the water and play, splashing around like a little child. Mother sits on a blanket under an umbrella, and watches from the shore. She waves as the waves wash over me. She looks like she does in her old faded pictures, when she was a young beauty queen, filled with dreams and hope for the future. Now they're just something to fill the pages of a dusty photo album stuffed in a drawer nobody opens anymore.

Then the tide comes in and starts sucking me out. I feel myself being drawn into the dark depths. I can see my mother screaming on shore. Other people come running. But I can't hear them. My ears are filled with ocean water.

I gasp, I flail. But to no avail.

I begin sinking. I can feel my lungs rapidly filling with liquid.

Then I see a light shining through the surface. I strive for it. I can almost touch it.

Then I'm back in her womb. I can't see her, but I can hear her. She is screaming in agony, but I don't know why.

Then the blood comes rushing in, I feel my life draining from me, and everything goes dark. I am finally at peace.

Teddy

I open my eyes. It's not over yet. Damn it.

But that's okay. I am afraid of the dark, anyway. Even though it offers me my only consolation.

At least I can still walk the dogs around the lake and through the woods. It is my only joy in life. That's all I ever want to do. Forever. That, or nothing. Just nothing. Like the dreamless sleep of my youth.

The dream I created is dying, though. I no longer want to fuck and kill. And that is all I ever do in the dream. There is nothing else to do.

But they are still looking for me. They cannot find me, not yet. I must keep moving. Hiding. Fucking. Killing. Dying. Then being born again. But not in a religious way, unless you mean reincarnation. I just want it to stop. But it keeps going. It is the proverbial vicious cycle.

I hug my teddy bear. I have had him since I was a child, carrying him with me everywhere, even when I am wandering the streets, homeless. It is the only remnant of my childhood that doesn't destroy me on a daily basis.

I tend to imbue inanimate objects with personalities. If they don't have souls, then neither do we, I willfully conclude.

I just want to wake up now. Or go to sleep. Either one, forever.

I am too tired to sleep.

Ephemeral Eternity

I am tied to the bed, being repeatedly raped by a hairy, drooling beast. His huge, throbbing member is cutting me in half, or so it seems. I cum despite my disgust, again and again, my tears blending with my blood. It still feels good, at least on the outside. So I stop struggling, and just let it happen. I don't care anymore.

Afterwards, he or it just leaves me there, dripping bodily fluids from every orifice. I hope I die. But I don't. Because it is only the dream. It may go on forever. There is nothing I can do to stop it now.

I just lie there passively, feeling my essence leak onto the sheets, soaking them with my liquidated soul.

I close my eyes and see my mother. She is sobbing, not smiling. So I open them again. My dreams are not as horrible as my memories.

A dog comes into the room, and chews the ropes, emancipating me. Together we track the monster rapist, and kill him, brutally, mercilessly.

It does not satisfy me. But it's something to pass the time, the endless hours of acute awareness.

I touch my own face, my own flesh. It feels real. Even in the dream. But that is part of the illusion. It is a deceptive sensation. It is how we manage to keep living, even though we all know we are going to die.

At least I hope so. Even though I am afraid of death. At least my own.

Sex is my only distraction. The dogs are my only salvation.

I want to take them with me when I finally disappear into the abyss. We will all find peace together, as a single, unified entity that no longer exists. That is my idea of "heaven."

Meantime, there is no escape from this prison. I must endure it until it decides to release me, even though I am innocent of any crime that would warrant such cruel punishment.

Nostalgia for the Future

While the present may offer coming attractions of the future, the future itself is often a mere remake of the past, and a poor one at that.

Sometimes during a listless lull, life is lucid. Then the clouds roll back in, and I am home again inside my dark cave, where time has no meaning, and nothing actually exists.

This is my comfort zone.

But even there, I can't stop thinking of what might've been. I am haunted by things that never happened.

This is why I invent my own past, because I cannot create my own future.

Dawn's Deception

When you first wake up sometimes, it's like you're rising from the dead. With the morning light comes that false sense of security, that phony feeling of relief, that fake optimism that wears off as the day goes on. Usually a morning like that follows a strange or traumatic evening. Depending on the event, this syndrome can last a minute or all day, and it seems as if nothing terrible has ever happened to you or anyone. Tragedy is the stuff of nightmares. You can't imagine dying. Ever.

Or killing someone. Someone you love. Even if it's a selfish act disguised as pity.

Compassionate Misanthropy

I am actually beginning to pity my own kind. Maybe it is because I feel myself slipping away from their ranks, and they will no longer bother me. But this new sense of empathy endangers my security, especially now that I am being followed, and watched, by unseen authorities.

I have a memory of a dream, or perhaps it actually happened.

I'm walking through Central Park with Mother. It is autumn and the ambience is spectacular and soothing. She is pushing a baby carriage. I look inside of it, and notice the baby has my face. It begins to cry.

Then I look up. Mother has vanished. It begins to rain, violently, with wind, thunder and lighting. The baby carriage is swept away. I am left behind, all alone.

That's all I ever remember.

I think of this dream or memory as I fuck my quarry all over town, in strange bedrooms, on rickety beds. We all cum at the same time. Then I let them go. Just like that. Safe and smiling with the sensual satisfaction that I gave them.

This new trend of mercy doesn't seem to be slowing down, but accelerating. I hate them, but I love to fuck them, and let them violate my body in all sorts of imaginative and hideous ways, all of which give me great pleasure. But the lust for post-coital death continues to elude me now.

I cannot afford compassion for my own kind. After all, it was never afforded me.

And look where I am now. Just look. Then tell me.

Have mercy on my soul. Take pity on me, as I have on you.

The authorities are closing in. I can feel them, sense them. But I do not fear them. I am ready.

Hawthorne Hills

It's a beautiful crisp and cool autumn day as Mother and I stroll together around our neighborhood, Hawthorne Hills in Seattle, just north of the University of Washington. We live in a charming midcentury modern home, made with wood and rock, painted aqua-green, our favorite color. We love the water.

The old homes are decorated with elaborate gardens, and we both marvel at the sumptuous flora and fauna, even as the tree leaves are turning brilliant colors. It is our favorite time of year.

As we walk, we talk about the upcoming holidays, and how we'll celebrate. We love Christmas and decorating the tree together. It's just so wonderful to be together again, after all that happened. We never thought it would be possible, except in a dream.

I am walking a dog as we stroll, a Husky. I think the dog is our pet, but it doesn't matter, because he (or she) is our friend. The Husky is very mellow and friendly to other dogs and people, even cats. From somewhere, beautiful music by Henry Mancini and Les Baxter is playing, filling the air with harmonious melodies.

The houses we pass seem filled with happy memories. None of which are ours. Who are these people? Why do they get to lead such tranquil lives?

It is a mystery that some explain by fate, or destiny, or karma. I have no explanation. It all seems like random luck to me.

That is why I enjoy the few moments when everything seems just right. Even if I'm only remembering something that never actually happened.

Suburban Swingers

I am fucking my ex-wife now. No wait, she is fucking someone else as I watch and masturbate. This is a game we play. I am not sure it's the morally acceptable thing to do, in fact I know it isn't, at least by conventional standards, but we both enjoy it. At least I do.

We always have our parties in our basement tiki bar. We have a cot there, but things get so wild, I usually just throw some blankets on the floor. They are so soiled after each session, I have to burn them and buy new ones. It's okay. I can afford it. I steal enough money to support our habits.

Sometimes I hire a bunch of black men to gang-bang her. I love watching their big black cocks penetrating her sweet, luscious pussy, making her cream over and over, screaming with release, her face streaked with tears of pain and pleasure.

Other times we pick up a comely female student at the University, and we both seduce her. Or I hire a few women from a classy escort service, and we all wine and dine before fucking and sucking each other.

My wife pretends to like it. I always make sure she has multiple orgasms, so it doesn't seem like this is all about me and my needs.

One day she calls me "insane." I have trouble denying it, but I still take offense, and I hit her, then fuck her until we both cum.

Eventually, this is how she becomes my ex-wife. We have many arguments, mostly about all the money I'm spending on our hobby, but also about my emotional and mental instability, as she sees it. And then one day, I kill her. Well, not directly. One of the greasy, dirty, ugly vagrants I pick up downtown and bring into our Hawthorne Hills home to feed before he fucks her for dessert, *he* kills her, while fucking her, and almost kills me before he runs away into the misty Halloween night. This trick has not turned out to be much of a treat.

I am too busy masturbating to notice what is happening, until it is too late. That is my story, anyway.

I cannot describe the vagrant to the police. For some reason, I can't remember his face. Or her face. It is all such a blur. Sometimes I wonder if he or she was ever there at all.

The police tell me they'd be back in touch, and not to leave town or anything. I get the impression I am a suspect.

I guess it looks suspicious, with my wife's bloody, butchered nude body lying spread eagle on the floor of our tiki bar basement, her luscious corpse soaking in a puddle of blood and semen and other fluids, including my own.

At first the cops can't believe such a beautiful woman could be my wife. But I show them our legal wedding certificate. This is Seattle. Anything is possible. Even a socially forbidden union like ours.

Even a pointless death like this. But then death is always pointless, just like life itself.

Isn't it?

So it ultimately doesn't matter what we do to fill the time in between the womb and the grave.

Does it?

You tell me. I just don't know. Or care. Not anymore.

Speak for yourself. That's what I'm doing. Even if I am only screaming inside a cerebral echo chamber.

Senseless Sensuality

After my wife's murder, I run away from home, to Seattle. Wait. I am already in Seattle. So I guess I don't run very far. I am ordered not to leave town, after all. But I don't report to the precinct as told, either. They've been after me ever since. Or so I assume. This is why I hide inside my dream, where they can't find me, and I can do whatever I want, with impunity. Even rape and murder, as either perpetrator, or victim, depending on my mood.

The media calls me a monster. But I am not a monster. They are. I'm not the one eating innocent dead animal flesh, am I?

In real life, I am only a dog walker. I have the license to prove it. Somewhere. How can I be persecuted and punished for crimes I commit when I am asleep? That is not fair. I am pretty sure it is not legal, either.

The reason I go on erotic binges and homicidal rampages in my dream is because my wife's murder traumatized my subconscious. At least that's what a shrink told me, until I kill him one day during a session, after he fucks me against my will.

I guess this proves his point.

When I walk around the streets, everyone seems so happy. That's when I decide they must die, so they can wake up and smell the truth about life in this world. It is not what it seems. It is only a dream.

Then it hits me. It's just a dream, which means I am free to do anything, to anyone, that I want.

So begins my kill-and-fuck spree. It brings me no joy or peace, but it passes the time while I sleep, in an exciting if unfulfilling manner.

Then I wake up and walk my beloved dogs, and rediscover the happiness that eludes me in the dream. If only I never had to sleep again. Or just sleep forever, but without any consciousness. I wouldn't know the difference, would I?

Neither will you.

Talk Show Therapy

Sometimes when I am younger I pretend I am on a celebrity talk show and I am watching myself on TV. I am in the company of big stars, because I am one of them. These are my famous friends. I have made my mother proud. I know she is at home, watching me. This makes me happy. I have accomplished my mission in life: to fulfill her own forgotten dreams.

The host asks me questions about my life. Some are meant to elicit amusing responses. But my answers are very troubling, because I am being truthful. The audience grows very quiet. The people sitting beside me grow uncomfortable. The host suggests we go to a commercial break.

This is how I know it is not really happening, because people with my story do not share it on celebrity talk shows. The censors would not approve. But even my dreams have sponsors, it seems.

I tell the host how my foster father abuses me and strangles my puppy right in front of me one day, just to punish me by killing something I love. He blames me for all the hardship in his life, including the death of his wife. She committed suicide before I came to live with him. I guess I am meant to be her replacement in his damaged heart.

But he is really just punishing himself, because he lost the person he loved most in life, and he blames himself for not giving her enough love to make her life worthwhile. He knows the puppy means more to me than anyone, even him. So he takes it away from me, that I may share in his interminable suffering.

It works. I have not been the same since.

I never even have a chance to take the puppy out for a walk before his little life is snuffed out.

I tell the host and the audience how my mother becomes mentally ill when I am conceived, and my real father cannot take the strain of raising me alone. He takes out his grief on me. Finally one day he kills himself, because he realizes he is the rightful target of his anger and sadness, not me. I am only a casualty of their copulation. Of course, I have no idea what happened to my real father. I just make up this story so I have some kind of explanation for his chronic absence.

Anyway, I don't care about him, whoever he is or was, nor do I care about any of my foster parents. I am much sadder about my poor dead puppy, buried in a shoebox. He or she was my true family. The audience laughs like they are not sure they are supposed to.

I don't care. That is the secret to survival both in life and in the dream: not giving a damn about anything or anyone.

Apathy works for me, anyway. At least until it doesn't. Then I am lost again, wandering the desolate streets of a city I do not recognize, without a TV to provide a portal into another dementia. I mean dimension.

Girl with an Umbrella

During my dog walks outside my usual jurisdiction, on the bridge running through Ravenna Park, a pretty little girl carrying an umbrella walks by me daily and bids me a pleasant hello. I nod politely in response, but never engage her in conversation. She is the only human that I ever feel safe enough around to make eye contact, but that's all I can share. Sometimes she is wearing a brightly colored dress with white socks and black shiny shoes. Other times, if it is warm and sunny, which is not very often, she is barefoot. But rain or shine, she always has the umbrella.

Though cheerful, she looks at the dog I'm walking with a wistful smile.

She seems familiar to me, and not just because I've become accustomed to seeing her on a regular basis. Finally I realize she looks exactly like old pictures of my mother when she was around the same age, ten or so.

As soon as I experience this epiphany, she vanishes from my route. It's like she never existed. That's how it always is with people and animals, though.

This represents to me the elusiveness of ultimate truth. Now you see it, now you don't. Once you think you have it in your grasp, it evaporates.

It's like when I strangle one of my victims in my dream, while we achieve simultaneous orgasms. Just when we both think we have all the answers, awareness of the secrets buried in our sensuality, they're gone. Nothing left to verify or validate. No epiphany, no resolution. Just a mess to clean up and toss out, like it was never there.

I miss the girl with the umbrella so much it makes me sob. The dogs try to comfort me. They know who she was, and what she really represented. They try to tell me, but I can't understand what they're saying.

Beautiful Horror

I enjoy watching horror films. They do not scare me. They inspire me. I get many ideas for my dreams from them. Murder is like sex because so many vital bodily fluids are spilled in the process of both killing and fucking. They are very similar acts of depravity.

Since all of the actors in all of the movies eventually die and only leave behind these phantom visages, all movies are eventually horror movies. I prefer the ones that don't pretend otherwise. I respect honesty, even when it hurts.

Throughout my childhood, I stay up late watching horror movies on TV in the places where I am raised, by numerous foster parents, after my mother tries to kill me while I am only an infant. But they are also abusive, the foster parents that is, both mentally and physically, so I am taken away from them too, eventually, after the damage is already done. Finally I just decide to make it on my own. I can do this because of my beauty, and my talent. At least for a while.

I use sex to get what I want. My mother teaches me this tactic, at least subliminally. Both women and men find me attractive. They do not love me. They only want to fuck me. So I fuck them back. We have an understanding. It's mutual contempt laced with lust.

But something is missing. I find it in the horror films. They soothe me, comfort me in my isolation from the rest of the world. I like the ones with lots of sex and gore. I bathe my brain in these bodily fluids, like a salve on an open wound, or liquid medication that coats one's stomach boiling in its own acid.

Then one day I realize that in my dreams, I can do anything they do in horror movies, and no one will catch me, because no one will notice, or care. Because none of them are real. Only I am real in the dream.

Soon I begin to doubt this, too. Perhaps I am only a dog walker by day, nothing more. That is okay. I would never hurt dogs anyway. They are my only friends, whether they are real or not. They don't know whether they're real, either. But they don't care.

I realize this is how to live: even if it's only a dream, it's important to love, and be loved. Otherwise life is not worth living, and the dream is not worth dreaming.

But I despise myself. I stare in the mirror at the face of a stranger. That is my true horror.

How to Make a Monster

Mother and I are watching a 1958 black-and-white horror film called *How to Make a Monster* on a dark, cold, rainy afternoon during one of my visits. She remembers seeing it as a young girl, in a movie theater. We are eating popcorn as we watch. Outside the window, autumn leaves swirl in the wind. This is as close to heaven as we get. Except when I'm walking a dog. But she's never around to share this with me. So we just watch old movies on TV.

She tells me the title of this movie should also be the title of her life story. Except I'm the monster, because she made me, not the other way around. I wonder about that sometimes, though.

I don't take offense. I understand. She regrets having me because she thinks my life is so screwed up and I'm only a dog walker. I didn't fulfill her lost dreams for her. But then she never expected me to.

Next we watch another old black-and-white movie called *Voodoo Woman*, from 1957. Mother thinks perhaps her illness is the result of a family curse, because she's from New Orleans.

I thought she was raised in Seattle. The setting of our story always changes, it seems. Only the plot remains the same.

The plot. Like the kind that entombs corpses. Our plot is merely a grave. We just need an epitaph for our shared tombstone.

We decide it's better left blank, because there is no way to give it poetry or romance. It is a horror movie without a title. And we're the only stars. We both just want it to end well. But it won't. We know this. We live with the awareness of our own mutually assured doom. There is no happy alternate ending to our shared story.

But at least we have each other.

Except I am beginning to suspect that one of us isn't real.

The Void

Horror movies don't scare me. But reality does, even if it's not really real.

When I am just a child, I never have dreams, except for fantasies about my future that never come to pass. At night, when I sleep, nothing happens. It is just dark. I have no consciousness of existence. I wonder if this is what death feels like: sensing nothing, not even one's self. Everything we can now perceive with our senses will suddenly vanish, sucked down the drain of the eternal abyss that is the true reality.

Is that so bad, if you don't know the difference?

I am afraid of finding out. I fuck and kill and then interrogate the beautiful naked corpses, probing for answers, but they do not respond. They have nothing to report from the other side. Because there is no other side, I suppose.

Could this be because once we die, there is nothing but an eternal black hole?

I begin to realize this is not a curse. It's mercy.

Still, it terrifies me, losing all consciousness, only because I would miss my dogs, even if I don't even know I am missing them. Who will take care of them? Maybe I should put them out of their misery first, before they're actually miserable. A preemptive strike against unbearable grief.

There does not seem to be any point to consciousness, except for distraction from inevitable oblivion.

I decide it is pleasure. So I indulge my senses in the dream, then destroy the evidence of my debauchery.

If we all disappear anyway, what difference does it make? We wake up from a dream only to find there was nothing else anyway.

Lycanthrope

Suddenly I am fucking a hairy man who drools on me. Or rather, he is fucking me. He has sharp fangs and claws, like a werewolf, with which he tears at my tender flesh. The erotic charge of being ravaged by a canine human is sensually overwhelming. I feel consumed, body and soul.

Then suddenly I am hovering over my own corpse, which is now being devoured by the very dogs I love.

I don't know which one is actually happening. Since both are horrible yet redeemed by something I love (savage sex, and the company of canines), it doesn't matter.

I just want both to stop. But they continue, simultaneously. One I am witnessing, the other I am experiencing. The pain and the pleasure are equally exquisite.

If you wait long enough, everything ends. That's the beauty and the sadness of consciousness.

Graffiti in the Rubber Room

Every day when I finish walking dogs, I go to my mailbox and find another letter from my mother. They are all neatly typed, though the content is haphazardly conveyed. Each reveals various vague death threats and conspiracy theories involving the FBI and UFOs. Sometimes she continues her rambling thoughts on the outside envelope, scribbled in ink, like graffiti.

If I had any shame, I would find this embarrassing. But I don't. Have any shame, that is.

At the top of each missive is an official letterhead from where she works as a secretary. The name of her place of improbable employment is the Cuckoo Clock Company.

The irony does not escape me. But I wish she could escape the irony.

She tells me in her letters that she hates this job but needs it to survive. They only hired her out of pity for the disabled.

I do not respond to these letters, because I have nothing to say to her anymore. I have nothing to say about anything now.

That is why I only communicate with canines, because we express ourselves with emotions that cannot be conveyed by words.

On my last day with her in Brooklyn, I take the train with her to the Cuckoo Clock Company in lower Manhattan, on my way to the airport.

She is very quiet and pensive. I do not speak either. The anticipation of my impending departure is saddening. I wipe away a tear from her cheek as we walk. I want to hug her, but it would be too intense for both of us. Our bond is unspoken, and untouchable.

She sits down at her desk and immediately starts typing. The office is depressingly generic and sterile, and yet eerie, like a ward for the insane.

Then she simply asks me to stop staring at her as she types, because it makes her nervous. And she is afraid of getting fired if I linger too long.

I kiss her gently on the forehead. "Goodbye," she says in a monotone. Her bluntness does not hurt me, because I know she is putting her emotions on autopilot, so she doesn't crash and burn.

Soon I will be just another phantom image in her tortured mind. Hopefully she considers my existence to be minor compensation for her epic woes. But I doubt it. I'm only a dog walker, nothing special. But hopefully my visit has given me some dimension in her consciousness, and a reason to continue.

How very vain of me.

I start to leave, suppressing tears, not sure I will ever see her again. In this version of reality, anyway.

Then she grabs me by the arm and tells me she'll be afraid when I'm gone. Not of crime, but of time. I tell her I love her, even though I'm not sure I mean it, and she thanks me. My empathy is all I have to give her. It is not enough to help her.

Notes from the Precipice

This is one of her letters, just to give you an idea. I save them all.

> *I was a beauty queen. I would've won the state as well as the city contest but I didn't want to sleep with anyone to get it. You think I am a whore but I am not. Mental illness is a terrible thing. Maybe you will get it too and you will know what I mean.*
>
> *Are you a faggot? My current husband is a faggot and a communist. Your father was a nigger. Or at least I think so. Maybe not. He had a huge cock anyway. He raped me. That's why you are here. I am sorry. I didn't want you. It's not my fault.*
>
> *But I had you anyway. You're welcome.*
>
> *I wandered the streets for years with only a suitcase. I was beaten and raped repeatedly. What's the point of anything?*
>
> *I hope you can come visit me one day and I will buy you some new clothes. What size do you wear? I would send you something for Christmas but I don't have very much money. I am poor. I have enclosed a copy of my check so you will not accuse me of being a liar as well as a whore. How dare you think such nasty things about your mother even if I didn't raise you I couldn't help it I'm ill.*
>
> *When I have more money I will send for you. I told your father I didn't want children but he raped me anyway. He's an asshole and so are you probably. I should've had an abortion. I'm sorry.*
>
> *I cannot support you so don't ask. I can barely take care of myself. If I marry a rich man I will give*

you money. Right now I am married to a Muslim terrorist. He has money but he won't give me any just enough for rent and groceries. He won't sleep with me because he's a faggot. I have to masturbate all the time because no one will fuck me anymore.

I was trained to be a great dramatic actress, not a receptionist. All of my skills have gone to waste. I had such promise. I hate where I work. It's very depressing. But now I'm too old and fat even to be a stupid model. I will be glad when I am dead. Dead people are so lucky.

When I move to Miami I will send for you. I should never have had you. I was abused now so are you. I feel sorry for you. Your life will be as tragic as mine. Don't forget that.

Come see me soon.

Macabre Masquerade

I decide I am not being followed. I am being watched, wherever I go. I know it. I feel their eyes on me, probing, dissecting, analyzing. I trust I am giving them a good show. At least someone is enjoying it.

I am not crazy, no more than any one of you. My pain is just more obvious than others. We all have our own unique disguises to mask our grief from the world.

I once saw a movie made in 1961 called *The Mask*. It was in 3D. The funny thing is, I wasn't wearing 3D glasses when I saw it. But that's how I experienced it, because the nightmare sequences set in Hell resonated with my own dreams. I don't need any special glasses. I just need the mask.

But I left my mask behind. In the womb. That is why I feel so naked and vulnerable in my waking world, since my true face feels exposed. It is the face of pure horror.

My mother wrote me once that my father raped her, so I am the byproduct of evil. She never wanted me. But she had me anyway. I should be grateful, she says.

I am not. No one else is, either, except maybe the dogs. But I have lived up to my mother's legacy of sin and sorrow. At least I can claim that much.

I hope I have made her proud. But I have no way of knowing, since she only exists in my mind now.

Sometimes I suspect I only exist in hers, too. That would explain a lot. Or excuse many of my actions, anyway. At least as far as my own consciousness or conscience is concerned. I don't know the difference between those two anymore, but it doesn't matter, because I am losing both.

Illusion Fusion

One day Mother and I go to the Grand Illusion Cinema in the University District to watch the 1962 horror movie *The Awful Dr. Orloff*. It is one of our favorites.

In one scene, the mad scientist is operating on an unconscious, kidnapped nude girl, strapped to a table in his secret lab.

Mother says the girl is *her*. Right now. As we are sitting here. She is the beautiful nude girl strapped to that table, being operated upon against her will because she is an unwitting captive of evil, and everything currently happening in what we both perceive to be our mutually experienced existence is merely a dream inside the head of the girl on the screen. Which is my mother's head. And when she wakes up, it will all end. If she wakes up, that is.

Or so Mother tells me. She also tells me the 1955 movie *Daughter of Horror* (AKA *Dementia*) is actually a documentary about her life – made before the fact, like a prophecy. Another old movie called *Night Tide*, from 1961, about a troubled young woman (Linda Lawson) that believes she is a mermaid in a carnival sideshow, is also based on Mother's own similar experience, at least according to her. And the 1957 movie *Blood of Dracula*, about a teenage female vampire, was inspired by her traumatic stay at a boarding school, which she likened to "a mental hospital."

I want to tell Mother about my own epic, cinematic, perpetually serialized dream. But now I am beginning to wonder whose dream it actually is, and if I am only a phantom in her dream, or she in mine.

Another time: my mother and I are up late one rainy night, watching a 1957 movie called *The Unearthly* on TV. I remark that she resembles one of the lead actresses, Allison Hayes, who died tragically young in real life.

Mother tells me it's because she used to be Allison Hayes. I find that hard to believe, and chalk it up to her colorful imagination, as I always do. But the resemblance is striking, at least when Mother was much younger. In fact, the other actress in the film, Sally Todd, is a dead ringer for my ex-wife, the one I murdered, at least psychically.

Mother doesn't believe my stories of horror any more than I believe hers, though. She claims I was never even married, because "perverts like me" are denied that right per society's pseudo-moralistic, hypocritical standards. I just made it up to justify my self-imposed solitude.

In the end, though, it doesn't matter what you believe, Mother always says to me. It's all bullshit anyway.

She has a point.

Piece of Mind

My mother is worried I will inherit her madness. I tell her not to worry, I am fine. I am simply a dog walker in real life. There is nothing wrong with me.

I am only crazy when I dream. But she doesn't need to know that. No one does.

As I've told you, per my research, I know that schizophrenia skips a generation. Well, that's what medical experts say, but they could be wrong. Why take the chance? My mother has often warned me that it is hereditary, a family voodoo curse, striking arbitrarily. I do not plan to procreate for this reason. I do not wish to bequeath this curse on an innocent child. This is why I never have sex in my waking world, since that might result in an unwanted child. I do not trust medical precautions.

I'd rather kill my baby in the womb than give birth to him. Or her. It would be a preemptive strike against certain tragedy, an act of mercy.

That's how I treat my victims in the dreams, even though I'm too late to prevent their misery. At least I cut it short for them. That's more compassion than I receive from this sadistic universe.

At least in my dream I can fuck, and be fucked, without consequence, like I can kill, but not be killed. Mutual pleasure is easier to attain than mutual pain, at least in the dream. In real life, it's the other way around.

This schism reminds me of a movie I once saw called *The Manster*, from 1959. An American businessman in Japan is subjected to experiments that result in a hideous extra head growing from his shoulder, driving him to commit heinous acts of hedonism, as I do in the dream. I often feel like I am being controlled by another mind, directing my actions against my will.

Maybe I am crazy. If so, I don't care. Insanity seems like the natural state of existence, since it's all so senseless. The pleasure is as pointless as the pain, because it's all fleeting, experiences reduced to memories that merge with dreams and imagination into a cerebral stew that ultimately gets flushed down the drain. Ultimately, none of it can be touched by the flesh, only felt by the mind, at least until the mind itself dissolves into nothingness.

But if the mind itself is ephemeral, what good are its contents? They will eventually disintegrate along with the gelatinous matter that encases them.

My thoughts and desires only live on in these words, words that no one will ever read. Except for you. And I am not even sure you are there.

Speechless

When describing Life's most precious moments, words are useless. They strain and primp and echo in the Void, but they cannot capture or record a mood the way a painting or a tune can.

Mere words can never convey the anguish of loss. Pain is often as indecipherable as beauty. The essence is always lost in translation. If only I could carry a tune or draw a picture for you.

But I have no aptitude for art and music. I only have words to express these things that I cannot touch, only feel.

And even that simple sensation is fading fast. Soon not even words will matter, because I will be in a place that has no language.

That sounds like heaven to me, especially after this hellish movie called Life. I must give it a soundtrack to make it bearable.

I look back over my life, not knowing which are memories and which are only dreams, and images float rapidly across my damaged mind in a continuous loop.

I can see my mother's face. It is smiling, but warped, like a cracked mirror.

I can see all the dogs I've walked, passing through time in a pastoral parade.

I can see the bodies of all my lovers, both before and after I killed them.

Sad music plays in my head as I watch. I can't look away. It's all I have left.

Silent Scream

No one can hear me anymore. Or else they just stop listening. So I stop talking to them. They don't seem to notice, or care. They ignore me even when they can obviously hear me, not even pretending to listen.

There is a song playing from somewhere, and everywhere. I think it's coming from inside my own head. "The Sound of Silence." But it is not being sung the way it was originally intended. It is being whispered, and then gradually, screamed. No one can hear it but me.

Emancipation Provocation

You may have noticed my field reports from both sides of the dream are growing shorter. Time is running out. My pursuers – or rather, my observers – are closing in on me. I can feel their looming, ominous presence constantly now.

I am slowly suffocating. Fading away, dissolving before my own eyes. Soon it will all be over. Life goes by faster the longer you live it. It's like it can't wait to end.

Moments are memories before you can even appreciate their place in your life, or rather, your brief existence, and memories are souvenirs of a journey that never takes you to your original destination.

But then I can only speak for myself, to whoever will listen. Even if it's just you.

Cul-de-sac

I know it's all over when suddenly I again see the little girl with the umbrella – but not on the Ravenna Park Bridge while I'm walking a dog in my waking life.

I see her in the dream.

The boundaries have been breached. I am no longer safe within the confines of my own broken brain. The outside world has invaded.

She is not carrying a pretty umbrella, but instead wearing an ugly yellow raincoat. Her face is ghoulish now, her flesh decaying and gray, her pupils obscured by mucous infused cataracts. She is pointing at me and smiling as always. But this time she isn't radiating love and happiness. She is grimacing with malevolent malice, exposing rotting, jagged teeth. She has been the one following me all along, across dimensions of time and space, into the dream, my former sanctuary. The authorities are behind her. She has led them to me.

This is the end. At last. I am afraid, but ready.

Awakening

I suddenly remember it all in a rush, memories and dreams flowing together in a single current, rather than twin, parallel tributaries leading to the endless black sea. My life passes before my eyes, like a horror movie on fast forward. I have already mentally rewound my life so many times it feels worn out, like an overplayed videocassette tape, which is an archaic format. Like me.

I am living on the streets, penniless and alone, until the rape, when the officials in charge of my destiny decide to give me free room and board in exchange for my freedom. I am formally declared a ward of the state because I am considered a danger to society. The world that destroyed me deems me a threat to its stability. Irony is a bitch.

Instead of treating me with compassion, the authorities tell me I am insane. They claim I am suffering a sudden, psychotic break from what they deem as "reality," after a hideous, hairy, homeless man rapes me one cold, dark night, and I become unwillingly impregnated. This violent biological aberration coincides with the onset of my mental illness, which some designate as "schizophrenia."

I identify it as "acute awareness." But my self-diagnosis goes unheeded by the self-proclaimed experts treating me, or imprisoning me.

Doctors determine my mental illness is due to a latent gene, triggered but not caused by my trauma. I do not want to pass this curse on to my baby. The innocent among us must be protected from our disease as a species. We are a plague upon this planet. Nothing changes that fact.

After the abortion, I escape from the prison hospital by seducing then maiming one of the guards. I then begin to seduce total strangers of all sexes in bars, bus depots and alleys, only to fuck and kill them. I make my living as a prostitute, not a model. There is no difference in these occupations from a practical point of view. We use our sex to survive in a harsh world.

The authorities have it all wrong. They assert I was never a homicidal sex fiend on the loose, except within the confines of my own malfunctioning mind. I never hurt anyone. I never even walked any dogs, not since my real father murdered my puppy after my real mother committed suicide, because he blamed her death on me. Neither did my son, or daughter, whichever it might've been, because he or she was never actually "here." Somehow I conflated his or her fabricated identity with my own, and then imagined an alternative reality – several, in fact. Memories merged with dreams and imaginary visions. Isn't that the definition of life itself?

But none of it actually happened, or so they try to convince me. I've been trapped in this white, cold, antiseptic room the whole time, ever since the rape, which happened after living on my own for many years, after my husband abandoned me, for the crime of chemical dysfunction. So I killed him, but nobody knows that. They think he killed himself. It was not my choice, not my fault. My condition, I mean. And yet it cost me everything. And everyone. My unborn child is merely collateral damage of a death sentence that took a lifetime to fulfill.

The "room" I refer to is really inside my skull, or so they say. And this "confession" is simply the graffiti all over the rubber walls, scribbled in my own blood, at least I think it's mine. My only escape from this asylum of flesh is within my own feverish imagination, creative byproducts of a degenerative disease.

It doesn't matter now what was real and what was fantasy. They're both over now. Only one eternal truth endures, outliving them both. Outliving us all.

They say that creativity is simply sublimated madness, and artists are merely maniacs that have mastered the ability to assimilate into society. I suppose I have failed as both an artist and a maniac. And even as a dreamer.

Every day I miss my boy or girl, the one that never had a chance to experience the beautiful horrors of this dream called Life. I justify my alleged crimes by imagining his or her life for him or her, one of overwhelming sorrow, naturally, but also fleeting if improbable tranquility, given his or her circumstances, which, like mine, were not of his or her choosing. I only remain alive this long for my aborted child's soul's sake, so he or she can live through me, even if it's only inside my dream, which the "experts" claim is merely a delusion. But now that's fading away along with my old, tired flesh.

I often write my phantom son or daughter letters I can never actually send, but he or she reads them anyway, because he or she exists only inside of my mind. And my mind is never very far away, even if I can't always locate it.

All human beings are willfully delusional, I tell my observers, but they don't believe me, due to their own hubris. They don't even hear me, since I have stopped talking. They will find out soon enough. I will take my awareness to my grave.

I welcome the darkness slowly enveloping me, because I know my son's or daughter's spirit is somewhere in that vast void. Meantime, I imagine he or she is thinking about me as he or she walks the dogs in a celestial limbo, until our inevitable rendezvous.

I am so sorry I could not give you a true life, my poor child, much less an illusionary one filled with joy and success. But I have no reference point in reality for those things, so I don't know how to conjure them for the sake of a fantasy. Even my imagination is broken. I hope the dogs I envisioned supplied you with the love I could never offer, and the sexual fantasies I concocted, however violent, fulfilled your base, sensuous desires. In that way, I lived vicariously through you, since my own memories of physical pleasure are murky and muddled by misery. You had a much better time than I ever could in these fantasies. All I could do was masturbate to them.

Outside the tiny window in my stark little room I see a double rainbow glowing like strips of psychedelic neon in a deep purple sky. The storm has passed. I don't know if this is an omen or just a coincidentally timed quirk of Nature, which is always open to personal interpretation, with no way to corroborate its true meaning other than blind faith. Things only mean what we want them to mean. But I will take it as a positive sign from beyond this realm, a benign beacon from the place where I am going right now, against my will, but without struggle.

For me, the nightmare is now over. The tormented spirits of dead dreams no longer haunt me.

I am finally awake.